Reed's Roar

In Honor of:
Reed Dewey

Dedication

To my beloved son, Reed Michael Dewey,
Your short but profound life story is the inspiration behind this book.
Mommy loves you forever, my Reedy boy.

Acknowledgment

I am deeply grateful for the unwavering support and
encouragement
of my husband, Eric, and my parents throughout the
process of writing this personal and meaningful
children's book.
I pray it touches the hearts of all who read it.

This is a story about a little cub named Reed.
He loved to laugh, play, and he was a joy to
be around, indeed.

His raspy roar was contagious, and his
giggles were outrageous!

Reed was sweet and special. His sweet grin
lit up every room he was in!

He was the youngest of three cubs.
All he knew was love, and all he gave was love.
He was truly sent from above.

There was nothing that Reed couldn't do.
He was kind, brave, curious, unique, and of
course, adorable, too.

But one day, a terrible accident happened to him.
One that left him very sore.
The doctors told him he'd have to lose his roar.

He was very sad.
Because you see, for lions, their roar is as essential
as a heartbeat.
So to lose your roar is no small feat.

Because of this sudden news,
He experienced a lot of emotions;
Enough to fill the oceans.

Reed felt confused and melancholy,
Which was the opposite of a cub who was
typically jolly.

The doctors had a plan.
They told him, "We will have to remove your
roar, but we will try and preserve it if we can."

Then, Reed came up with an idea... and he
pondered, "I wonder if there are any other cubs
out there that could benefit from me?
I'll have the doctors take a look and see."

He thought, "If my roar is still fine, maybe I
can give it away.
Yes, even though it's technically mine."

He talked to his parents, and they agreed.
His roar no longer could serve him, but they
were so proud of their Reed.

ROAR

His roar was, in fact, wonderful.
He was happy to see that it was as healthy as
could be. It was still raspy and sweet, like it never
skipped a beat.

He told the docs, 'Please find a cub who's
needing a roar,
Since I won't get to keep my own anymore.'

He said, "I may have to lose my roar, but I don't
want this loss to be in vain.
For I bet there are cubs out there who also feel
this pain...

Some cubs don't even have a roar...
So if I can donate mine, they'll thrive even more!"

He decided to give his roar to someone in need.
It was a brave idea, and such a selfless deed.

Reed's family was so proud of him for being so
generous.
They knew it was a hard thing to do,
But they learned by doing this that he'd feel better, too.

I can't wait to roar again

For it's more of a blessing to give than to receive.
Even when the circumstances are hard to perceive.

Once the doctors found a fellow cub who was in
need, Reed said, "Let's go give it to them. I'll take
the lead!"

This little cub was so grateful that Reed made such
a brave choice.
She hugged him tight.
She said, "This may not have been an easy
decision, but it was right."

She and her family thanked him for giving her his roar. With happy tears, she said, "I feel no pain anymore."

Though Reed was no longer able to roar like he used to, he still made the best of what he did have. He had his family and a whole lot of love.

He helped another cub, and that made his heart happy...

Because of the magnitude of his sacrifice, it was hard not to be sappy.

Because of Reed and his roar, that little cub got a
chance to live a happier life.
She can now roar, and when she does, she feels the
joy that Reed had, right down to her core.

Reed and his family hoped that this great gift
Would create a positive shift—
something so priceless,
Like giving life to the lifeless.

So, if you ever have the chance to help those in need,
we sure hope you do and that you'll think of Reed.

About the Author

My name is Lindsay Dewey. I am a stay—at—home wife and mother, living in Idaho with my family.

I wanted to share the backstory of this book. It is written in honor of our youngest child, Reed. In February 2025, just shy of 22 months old, our sweet boy was involved in a sudden and tragic accident at home, which resulted in the end of his life. He sustained a traumatic brain injury and went to be with Jesus the day before Valentine's Day.

We made the decision to donate his perfectly healthy organs so that another family would never have to experience the pain of losing their child. After all, he didn't need them anymore—he had a new and restored body in Heaven. Reed's perfect little body saved lives by donating five vital organs to other people in need: three children and one adult.

This book is about bravery, sacrifice, and kindness. I wanted to write a story to honor Reed's life—to bring beauty and inspiration from ashes. The lion character, including his clothing, is inspired by Reed's beloved "lovey" blanket that he carried with him everywhere.

Reed was the most adorable, sweet, and fun little boy. He was deeply cherished by his parents and his two older siblings. He radiated joy and spunk, constantly kept us on our toes, and had a special way of charming us and making us laugh. All he knew was love, and all he gave was love.
We miss him so deeply, but we know we will spend eternity with him in Heaven. His life has touched millions of people around the world, and I hope his story inspires you to be kind, brave, selfless, and to help those in need whenever you can.
This story was lovingly written to help you Remember Reed.

"And don't forget to do good and to share with those in need. These are the sacrifices that please God."

— Hebrews 13:16

In Loving Memory of
Reed Michael Dewey
April 25, 2023 – February 13, 2025

The End